Rumblewick's ~~My~~ DIARY ②

MY Unwilling WITCH
starts a girl band

Hiawyn Oram * **Sarah Warburton**

ORCHARD BOOKS

A SHORT HISTORY
OF HOW YOU COME TO BE READING MY
VERY PRIVATE DIARIES

In a snail shell, they were STOLEN. Oh yes, no less. My witch Haggy Aggy (HA for short) sneaked into my log basket and helped herself.

According to her, this is what happened:

On one of her many shopping trips to Your Side she met a Book Wiz. (I am told you call them publishers, though Wiz seems more fitting as they make books appear, as if by magic, <u>every day</u> <u>of the week</u>.)

Anyway, this Book Wiz/publisher wanted HA to write an account of HER life as a witch here on Our Side. Of course, HA wasn't willing to do <u>that</u>. Being the most unwilling witch in witchdom, she is far too busy shopping, watching telly, not cackling, being anything BUT a witch and getting me into trouble with the High Hags* as a result.

The Book Wiz begged on her knees (apparently) and offered HA a life's supply of shoes if she came up with something. So HA did. She came up with THIS — MY DIARIES. ALL OF THEM!!!!

Of course, when I wrote the diaries, I was <u>not</u> expecting anyone to read them. Let alone Othersiders like you. But as you are, here is a word to the wise about how things work between us:

* The High Hags run everything round here. They RULE.

1. We are here on THIS SIDE and you are there on the OTHER SIDE.

2. Between us is the HORIZON LINE.

3. You don't see we're here, on This Side, living our lives, because for you the HORIZON LINE is always a day away. You can walk for a thousand moons (or more for all I know), but you'll never reach it.

4. On the other paw, we know you're there because we visit you all the time. This is partly because of broomsticks. A broomstick has no trouble with any Horizon Line anywhere. A broomstick (with one or more of us upon it) just flies straight through.

And it has to be like that because scaring Otherside children into their wits is part of witches' work. In fact it is Number One on the Witches' Charter of Good Practice (see copy glued at the back).

On the other paw, it is NOWHERE in the Charter for a witch to go over to Your Side to make friends and try to be and do everything you are and do — as my witch Haggy Aggy does.

But then, that's my giant problem: being cat to a witch who doesn't want to be one. And as you will see from these diaries, it makes my life a right BAG OF HEDGEHOGS. So all I can say is, if HA tries to make friends with YOU, send her straight back to This Side with a spider in her ear.

Thank you,

Rumblewick Spellwacker Mortimer B. xxx

THIS DIARY BELONGS TO:

Rumblewick Spellwacker Mortimer B.

RUMBLEWICK for short, RB for shortest

ADDRESS:
Thirteen Chimneys,
Wizton-under-Wold, This Side
Bird's Eye View: 331 N by WW

TELEPHONE:
77+3-5+1-7

NEAREST OTHERSIDE TELEPHONE:
Ditch and Candleberry Bush Street,
N by SE Over the Horizon

BIRTH DAY:
Windy Day 23rd Magogary

EDUCATION:
The Awethunder School For Familiars
12-Moon Apprenticeship to the
High Hag Witch Trixie Fiddlestick

QUALIFICATIONS:
Certified Witch's Familiar

CURRENT EMPLOYMENT:
Seven-year contract with Witch Hagatha Agatha,
Haggy Aggy for short, HA for shortest

HOBBIES:
Catnastics, Point-to-Point Shrewing, Languages

NEXT OF KIN:
Uncle Sherbet (retired Witch's Familiar)
Mouldy Old Cottage,
Flying Teapot Street,
Prancetown

Dear Diary,

In a zillion moons you will never guess where I am writing this, so I'll tell you — on the Other Side in an enormous bed in The Righton Luxury Beach Hotel!!!

We are here because Haggy Aggy saw it on TV.

"Everyone deserves a lot of luxury once in their lives, RB," she said. "And witches and their Familiars are no exception. Now let's get packing and go."

We did not go at once. In fact, we did not leave for

TWO DAYS

because she couldn't decide what to pack.

Her biggest problem was what to wear on the luxury beach and beside the 'dazzling ultramarine' pool.

I mean.
I ask you.

A witch on a beach or beside a pool — luxury and dazzling or just plain wet and bedraggling? Not in the Witches' Charter of Good Practice, that is for sure.

<u>And</u> if the High Hags see HA in swim wear AT ALL, I know what they will certainly do. They will certainly send me back to First Grade in Witch's Cat School to relearn how to keep my witch from showing her knees and getting herself deep in cold water.

Meanwhile, as I write, HA is downstairs — in her words — enjoying a drink in the Pink Fizz Lounge.

"I shall also be socialising," she said, "which for your edification means making friends with Othersiders. You see, this is what one does when one comes to a luxury beach hotel like The Righton.

It is expected."

She wanted me to socialise with her but
I wriggled out of it because of

the stares.

I just had to have a break from

 the stares.

Everywhere we go in this place, the other
Luxury Breakers look at us as if we had
three heads. SOCKS! I'll have to hide you.
She's at our door, rattling the key card in
the key card slot and singing
FLY ME TO THE TOP OF THE
HIGHEST TOWER at the

top of her voice!

Dear Diary,

What a day it has been at The Righton.

After a stare-filled lunch (well, HA's hat WAS bigger than an alien wizard's flying saucer), she was attracted by a sign near the hotel entrance. "Oh, RB!" she cried. "Do look! It's covered in glitzy stars so it must have something **very** important to communicate. Now you read Otherside better than I do, so read it to me,

<u>please</u>, at the triple pre<u>sto</u>!"

So I did and in between the STARS it said:

GIRL BANDS ARE US

WE MAKE THEM BIG.
COULD YOU BE OUR NEXT
BIG ONE?
AUDITIONS START AT 15.00 hrs
IN THE STARSTRUCK ROOM
ON THE FIRST FLOOR.
BE THERE AND BE BIGGER THAN
YOU EVER DREAMED
YOU COULD BE.

14

At that point we did not know what a Girl Band or a Girl Band audition was but HA insisted we went up to the Starstruck Room to find out.

And find out we did: a Girl Band is Otherside girls dressing up (or wearing clothes that nearly fall off), dancing on a shiny platform and singing like their voices just jumped out of their bodies and got dancing too.

An audition is when a Girl Band does all the above in front of three Othersiders who are called the Producers and Promoters.

When the PPs have watched many Girl Band auditions over many moons, they will choose the band they like best and make it 'bigger' than it ever dreamed it could be.

And being **bigger** than you ever

dreamed

you could be means

1 dancing and singing on TV and shiny platforms all over the universe,

2 having zillions of your songs heard by Othersiders in what they call ALBUMS,

20 Zillion Album Sales

3 appearing on pocket-sized TVs that Othersiders keep close at all times (and also use for non-stop talking to OTHER Othersiders probably because they don't have broomsticks to get there and talk for real).

Well, no prizes for guessing what HA is going to do now.

Oh YES!

The moment we left the Starstruck Room, she announced it.

She is going to
start her own Girl Band.
And enter it in the next

GIRL BANDS
ARE US

audition in seven days' time!!

WARNING
TOP
SECRET

And here,
dear Diary, is
where I am going to
make a CONFESSION because that's
what diaries are for — admitting the secret
thoughts you can't actually admit to
anyone else.

So this is it.
My secret confession:

I <u>LIKE</u> GIRL BAND MUSIC.

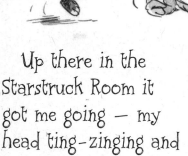

Up there in the
Starstruck Room it
got me going — my
head ting-zinging and
my paws tap-rapping.

And when my witch announced she was
going to start a Girl Band, I did not think
YUKSTRAW and TRIPLE YIKES, which any
proper Witch's Familiar should think.

I thought EXPLODING SUPERNOVAS and OVER THE MOON. THIS COULD BOIL AND BUBBLE!

Naturally, I did not admit any of this to HA. When we got back to our room, I did what I am trained to do when my witch strays from being a proper witch. I tried to talk her out of it.

"But, Haggy Aggy," I said, "you are not a girl; you are a witch. And witches are witches. They have no business in Girl Bands. And anyway, to start a Girl Band you need other girls. And you haven't got any other girls. Or perhaps you are thinking of asking Witch Understairs to join? Or maybe the High Hags?"

She did not notice my SARCASTIC tone, she was so carried away.

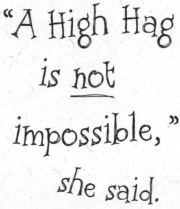

"A High Hag is _not_ impossible," she said.

"Especially the High Hag Iodine Underwood. I happen to know she has a BEAUTIFUL singing voice.

And in any case, I do have other girls for my Girl Band. I have Bella and

I have YOU!"

!! Bella and ME???!

!! ??

?

Now it was

YIKES AND THRICE YIKES.

"BUT," I protested, "Bella is a FROG.
A croaky green clinger! And ME?

I'm a highly qualified Familiar from

a long line of highly qualified Familiars.

I AM NOT,
and NEVER CAN be,
a girl in a Girl Band!"

"Rubble," said HA. "If there isn't
already a spell to turn you into a gorgeous
lookalike girl, you will invent one as soon
as we get home."

And with that she went to look for
more socialisation opportunities in the
Pink Fizz Bar, and this time she didn't
even ask me to go with her.

00014987

'BORN WITH CLOTHES ON'
LIVE IN CONCERT
At
OLYMPUS STADIUM
Gates Open 5pm - Concert 7.45pm
Dolmat Stand - Upper

BLOCK	ROW	SEAT
C	0	23

Enter Via Turnstiles 45 to 50

Dear Diary,

We are back home from The Righton
and the situation has not improved
a tiddly tadpole.

HA is out right now at a concert by
a Girl Band called BORN WITH
CLOTHES ON. A Girl Band that is
apparently already 'big'.

And guess what? She's only taken — not
me but — Bella!

"I need to see what 'big' is," she said.
"And what 'big' wears. And I'm
taking Bella because SHE has
such a good eye
for style."

(A good eye for a
bubbling, boiling cauldron
if you ask me. I mean.
You should SEE how that
frog slimes up to HA.)

"But don't worry, RB," she went on, "while we are gone there is SO MUCH for you to do. First you are to come up with a spell to turn yourself into a Girl Band Girl Lookalike. And when you've done that I want you to come up with a dazzling NAME for our band and write us

a WINNING SONG

for our audition. And I know you will because that's what you do — whatever I ask of you."

Well, what a nest of nettles! It IS in my Contract of Service to obey my witch's every whim and word, come fire, brimstone or alien wizards invading.

But there is just <u>NO WAY</u> I am <u>EVER</u> going to be a GIRL in a GIRL BAND.

I mean. I ask you. Leaving out what the High Hags would do if they caught me,

I HAVE MY <u>PRIDE</u>.

But don't worry, Diary, an idea is coming to me. Yes, here it comes winging its way like a screech owl:

I'll invent a

Girl Lookalike spell
in TWO LAYERS.

One <u>layer</u> for HA's eyes with a second <u>layer</u> that is the REAL SPELL — INVISIBLE unless you know it's there.

And the un<u>der layer</u> — where the ACTUAL SPELL lies — will do the following: it will turn the One To Be Spelled (in this case me, worst luck) into a Girl Lookalike all right — a Girl Lookalike who HA wouldn't want in her Girl Band if she was the last girl in the **world!!**

BRILLIANT

– though I say it myself.

Dear Diary,

I've done it — though it hasn't yet been tested because someone else has to perform it on me. (Invented like that so HA can never accuse me of not performing it properly on myself, on purpose.)

Here is the top layer that covers
the real spell:

THE LOOK-LIKE-A-GIRL-BAND-GIRL SPELL

Drape the shoulders of the OTBS (One To Be Spelled)
with a pink feather thing. Stand in your hat wearing
a pair of high teeterers and holding a cracked mirror.
Turn full circle three times without falling over while
turning the cracked mirror to face the OTBS and chant:

Who looks on you will look and see
A girl in trousers tight
Whose face and legs and arms and all
Are such a pretty sight
For when I step out from this hat
You'll give a girlish twirl
And those who look will look and see
A GORGEOUS GIRL BAND GIRL!

SMALL PRINT: This is a First-Chance-Last-Chance Spell.
If it doesn't work the first time, it never will and no other
Look-Like-A-Girl-Band-Girl Spell will either.
Bad luck but that's magic for you.

REVERSAL NOTE: Easy reversal is built into this spell.
To reverse at any time, the One Who Has Been Spelled should sneeze
three times at the moon and shout his/her full name followed by <u>THAT TIS I</u>

And here is the secret 'under layer' — where the REAL spell and its workings lie!

THE LOOK-LIKE-A-GIRL-BAND-GIRL SPELL

WHO LOOKS LIKE A TOAD IN TIGHT TROUSERS

Drape the shoulders of the OTBS (One To Be Spelled) with a pink feather thing. Stand in your hat wearing a pair of high teeterers and holding a cracked mirror. Turn full circle three times without falling over while turning the cracked mirror to face the OTBS and chanting:

Who looks on you will look and see
A girl in trousers tight
Whose face and legs and arms and all
Are not a pretty sight
For when I step out from this hat
Though in a girl-like mode
Who looks on you will more like see
A TIGHTLY TROUSERED TOAD!

SMALL PRINT: This is a First-Chance-Last-Chance Spell.
If it doesn't work the first time, it never will and no other
Look-Like-A-Girl-Band-Girl-Spell will either. Bad luck but that's magic for you.

Did I hear you say, "Good work, RB," Diary? I think I did.

And that done, I can get on with the thrills and spills part — coming up with a supernova name and writing a winning song for a Girl Band that thankfully I'll never be in!!

So, the name?

The name,

the name,

the name???

I heard the GIRL BANDS ARE US Producers and Promoters say they are looking for something different. Well, nothing could be more different than HA's Girl Band as it's not a GIRL Band.

It's a Witch And Frog Band with maybe a High Hag or two in it. So why not hit them with the truth which is always bigger than anything else.

SO, POSSIBLE NAMES FOR
HA'S GIRL BAND:

The Witch, the Frog and the High Hag(s)

The Toadstools

The Potions

The Spell Sisters

The Fireflies

Boil and Bubble

Boiling It Big

Cold Comfrey

The Witch Watch

The Hey Prestos

The Wizton Wonders

The Wizton Wailers

The Crooning Coven

Bubbling Over

the Spell SISTERS

SPELLSISTERS

the POTIONS

THE FIREFLIES

All In Black

Witch's whiskers! Now that would work getting her back into black...

The Blue Moons

Once In A Blue Moon*

No Ordinary Girls

The Never Ever Girls

Forever Witches

The Cauldron Stirrers

~~No Ordinary Girls~~ (got that already)

Bewitching Sisters

The Fire and Brimstones

Oh, SOCKS.

This is fun and

there's the doorbell!

Continue soon.

*I like this

Dear Diary,

My best friend, Grimey — that's who it was.

Total moon that he is, when I'd told him the whole Girl Band saga, he offered to help me invent a winning song.

Of course neither of us had invented a song before, but we decided it couldn't be that different from inventing a spell.

And as it turned out,

it wasn't.

First we decided we had to sing about something that mattered to us. And, as he is my greatest friend in the universe and I am his, what better than <u>that</u> for a song subject — friendship???

So we dusted down a witch's horn and a gawbox that have been under the sofa for moons.

I dug out my school washboard. We turned over a few cauldrons to drum on with stirring sticks and LET IT HAPPEN. And I have to admit, I can't remember when I've enjoyed myself MORE!!

This is what we came up with.
It's called BE RIGHT THERE:

A friend's a friend you have to win
Now I have through thick and thin
You'll be my friend, my total moon,
I'll be right there
whatever —

If you feel blue I won't be too
I'll dig right in and root for you
If you need time to be alone
I'll keep away and stay at home

If you are riding far too high
And lose your way, I'll come, I'll fly
And be right there
be right there, be right there
whatever —

A friend's a friend you have to win
Now I have, through thick and thin
You'll be my friend, my total moon
I'll be right there
whatever —

If you have crossed a line too far
And can't remember what you are
If you have fallen in a hole
To get you out will be my role

If every spell you do goes wrong
And you can't see where you belong
I'll be right there
        be right there, be right there
            whatever —

A friend's a friend you have to win
Now I have, through thick and thin
You'll be my friend
    I'll be right there
        be right there, be right there
            forever!

WHAT DO YOU THINK??

Anyway got to go — by the sound of it,
HA and the Clinger are home!

Much Later, In My Log Basket

Dear Diary,

Well, this is what happens when
a Familiar and his witch get carried
away with business that is not their
business like song-writing and Girl Bands:
Trouble comes knocking.

In this case Trouble in the form of the
High Hag Iodine Underwood — the one with
the beautiful singing voice.

First, though, before she arrived, HA and
the Clinger came dancing in through the
door full of the songs they'd heard at the
concert and what HA is going to wear as
the No. 1 singer in her own Girl Band!

And wait for it, Diary. Wait for it.

BLACK.

Oh yes, no less. HA has discovered that black is big in Girl Bands — and now she's talking as if she never said, "Black is yesterday, pink is the new black." Now she has packed all her pink in her flying trunk and sent it to the broomstick shed!!!

She told me to go get some black which she quickly cut about with the kitchen scissors — pulled on some cliff-high white boots and there she was looking all

Girl Bandish
back in
black!!!

I couldn't believe it. THEN, when I got out my list of possible names for her band, she didn't even LOOK at it.

"Don't worry, RB," she said, "flying home from the concert, Bella and I came up with the dazzling band name we need. It's obvious, isn't it:

'BACK IN BLACK!!'"

They were so excited they did not
see my disappointment that my list of
names was not needed or listen when
I said, "That's almost the name I was going
to suggest."

HA did not ask if I'd invented a Look-
Like-A-Girl-Band-Girl Spell. NOR
did she ask if I'd written
a winning song. Why? Because
she and Bella had not only
come up with the name
for the band on their
way back from the
concert — but
a song too.

"And it's so HOT it's MAGMA!"
cried HA. "LISTEN!"

Well, you could
have knocked me over with a pink
feather thing. HA was right. Their song
boiled and bubbled. It steamed. It WAS
magma — straight from the volcano's
mouth! I could just hear it winning any
audition and making HA bigger than she'd
ever DREAMED she could be.

It goes like this:

BELLA: RIBBIT, RIBBIT

HA: YOU CAN'T INHIBIT...................ME

BELLA: RIBBIT, RIBBIT...

HA: STAR EXHIBIT...................ME
Like a star in the heavens
I'm a light on the ground
My time's been a-coming
Now my time's come around

BELLA: RIBBIT, RIBBIT, RIBBIT, RIBBIT

HA: Yeah, I'm hot, hot rocking
In my little black dress
If the world is watching
I can only confess...

BELLA: RIBBIT, RIBBIT — CAN'T INHIBIT...
HER RIBBIT, RIBBIT...

```
BOTH:     STAR EXHIBIT.....................ME/HER
          Yeah...we're hot, hip hopping
          In our high, high heels
          Let the world get watching
          And know how it feels...
          RIBBIT, RIBBIT
          RIBBIT, RIBBIT — STAR EXHIBIT...

HA:       ME!
```

When they'd finished I was so amazed, I didn't know what to say. And it didn't matter because this was the moment when Trouble/the High Hag Iodine Underwood rapped on the window and demanded to be let in!

Oh! What's this? It's Bella the Clinger hopping towards my basket, sobbing a pond. I'll go on later —

if I don't drown in her tears.

Nearly Dawning Time And Sorry If You're Soaked

Dear Diary,

Bella was sobbing a pond
because she isn't going to be in
HA's Girl Band after
all — but I'll come to that in a moment.

Meanwhile, back to the entrance of the
High Hag Iodine Underwood.

I smelt wet rot immediately — because it
turned out she hadn't come to roast HA for
hot, hot rocking in a little black dress — or
me for letting her.

She'd heard the singing on her way to
take comfrey with Witch Understairs next
door. Said she hadn't let her voice out for
moons and could she *JOIN IN????*

So join in she did. And blow me down
with a feather thing again, can she sing?
She can belt it out and rock with the best.
She can also play the horn and the gawbox!
    And with me on the cauldron drums,
Thirteen Chimneys was soon jumping so
hard its Thirteen Chimneys

were rocking too.

When we'd done STAR EXHIBIT a few times, Underwood announced, "One song doesn't make a band, Hagatha dear. So do you have anything else original we can sing?"

HA pointed at me and said, "RB has invented a winning song,

HAVE YOU NOT,

BECAUSE I TOLD YOU TO."

So I sang through BE RIGHT
THERE and even HA thought it was
pretty hot. By the time we'd sung it
together a few times, Witch Understairs
and Grimey arrived to find out what was
going on. So did all the frogs from the frog
pen, all the eavesdroppers AND Witch
Rattle and her friend Witch Sideways PLUS
their Familiars, Arbuthnot Butnot and
Magic Galore — on their way home from
The Blue Moon Comfrey Rooms.
And everyone agreed on this: we were
too good
to waste.

Too good not to be heard by a wider audience. And would we PLEASE perform at the next Witches' Conference and every Witches' Jamboree forever???

At this point I saw the **Trouble** we were in showing itself like the mouth of a deep abyss.

HA started to sheer.

Sheer at the very idea that her Girl Band was meant for witches' conferences and jamborees — and not for much bigger things like winning the Girl Bands Are Us competition — and disappearing from witchdom for ever because she'd become an Otherside Girl Band so big it was galaxy-sized!

Luckily, Underwood stopped her before she really got started. "Oh, thank you everyone for your high praise indeed. But, as a High Hag, I can NEVER be seen performing in a witch band. The other High Hags would consider it Silly and therefore

Undermining High Hag Authority and for
SILLY and UNDERMINING HIGH HAG
AUTHORITY, a High Hag is sent spinning
into The Blue That Lies Beyond All. So now
I'll put my voice back in its box and we'll
forget this evening
ever happened!"

With that she cast
a cloud of Polished Talon Dust
about the room to make us
forget what we'd seen.

HA and I were quick
enough to avoid any of it
falling on us. But the dust
showered down on the others and as
soon as Underwood had left, they started
wondering what they were doing in
our house.

HA sent them home with no
explanation other than 'witnessing
the birth of 'BACK IN BLACK', which made
as much sense to them as if she'd said

JIBBLES and JIRASOLES.

And as soon as we were on our own,

HA exploded

with excitement — and I saw

just how deep the Abyss of Trouble

was that we were

about to fall into.

"Oh, RB, Bella...

don't you see..."

she cried.

"I've found the other girl for my Girl Band. It's HER. Iodine Underwood! She sings like a skylark. And she hot rocks too. With that voice and my voice, BACK IN BLACK can't fail to become galaxy-sized. Now, here's the challenge. How are we going to make her look <u>NOT</u> like the horrendous old Hag she is but a gorgeous Girl Band Girl?"

She paced about in her cliff-high boots and then spun round and pointed at me.

"Easy. Of course. While we were at the concert, you came up with a LOOK-LIKE-A-GIRL-BAND-GIRL SPELL.

Didn't you?

Because if not,

why not?"

The spell — with its double
layers — was lying on the kitchen table.
I tried to get to it, thinking...turning a High
Hag into a girl that looks like a toad in
tight trousers WOULD NOT BE A GOOD
MOVE for a witch and her Familiar.
But HA's beady eyes went ahead of me.
"Of course, you did.
Because you are the
most faithful
Familiar ever to
come out of
Familiar
School."
And she pounced
on it. And flicked
through it — naturally
only seeing its
surface layer.

"Tempests and treacle, this will do the trick, perfectly!"

she declared. "Now all I have to do is visit High Hags' Headquarters and perform it on Iodine. Thank you, RB."

"But-but-but," I stammered.
"You mustn't.
You can't.

That spell has...I don't think it's...it hasn't been tested."

"So now we'll test it," said HA. "Bring me a superspeedy broomstick that I won't feel sick on, RB. I must do this alone."

"No, no, HA," I argued. "It's too dangerous. If the other High Hags find a Girl Band Girl Lookalike in their Headquarters, what'll they do? Find out who put her there — YOU — and chase you into the byways and back alleys of witchdom, or worse: turn me into

a cauldron <u>toad</u> for <u>letting</u> you!"

"And, and," added Bella, coming to my aid without knowing it, "if Iodine Underwood finds herself looking like a Girl Band Girl Lookalike, she'll know exactly who did it to her because of tonight."

"Right," I said. "Bella is right and so am I. Forget about the High Hag Iodine Underwood in your Girl Band."

"Besides," said Bella, "you don't need her. You have ME. And if you perform that spell on RB, you have him."

But HA was so carried away with herself as a galaxy-sized Girl Band, she forgot not to be cruel.

"YOU?" she almost cackled at Bella. "YOU? Compared to Iodine Underwood you don't sing. You <u>croak</u>. And as for you, RB, I've had second thoughts about you being in my band. You'll be far more useful taking care of us. Making sure we're produced and promoted right. Maybe inventing some more songs.

And becoming — how shall I put it — Back In Black's Manager Cat."

And here she presented me with a pair of eye shades, which she must have purchased at The Righton Beach Shop.

I put them on and have to confess again: a _thrill_ went through me.

My head spun.

Back In Black's Manager???

In eye shades. Strolling about in The Starstruck Room, negotiating my Girl Band's future with PPs?

Was this my destiny after all?

If it was, it wasn't crusty old vinegar. Not crusty old vinegar at all!

GALAXY-SIZED
GIRLBAND
MANAGER
OF THE YEAR

Dear Diary,

What webs we tangle ourselves in as soon as we try to be what we aren't. All I can say is I hope what has happened will be a lesson to me.

As soon as I put on those Righton Shop eye shades and thrilled at the thought of being Back In Black's Manager, I was sliding well into the

Abyss of Trouble.

And Sliding fast.

First, it came over me that HA was right. Iodine Underwood DID sing like a skylark who also rocks. HA is good and could pass for a gorgeous Girl Band Girl any day. But to win the GIRL BANDS ARE US competition we HAD to have Iodine in our band. (OUR band — note the slippery slide.) And as its new manager (in eye shades), I'd do anything to get her.

So, cool as a cauldron of hailstones, I told HA the truth about that Girl Lookalike spell. And then re-configured the spell —

at the presto —

to take out its <u>second</u> layer and make it work on its <u>surface</u> layer!!

76

"Just warn her,"
I said, "that if she refuses, you'll tell the other High Hags she

rocked

the night away at Thirteen Chimneys and she'll soon be sent SPINNING INTO THE BLUE THAT LIES BEYOND ALL."

Then I gave HA our speediest broomstick and wished her well on her mission.

What was I thinking,
Diary?

You tell me.
Because HA did just that.
And soon returned with Iodine
on the back of her broomstick
looking GORGEOUS
in her own little
black dress.

We kept her rehearsing here at
13 Chimneys (with plenty of reminders of
The Blue Beyond All) until the day arrived
for the auditions at The Starstruck Room.

Bella and I hung around at the back (I'd
made her my assistant to help with her
disappointment at not being in the band).

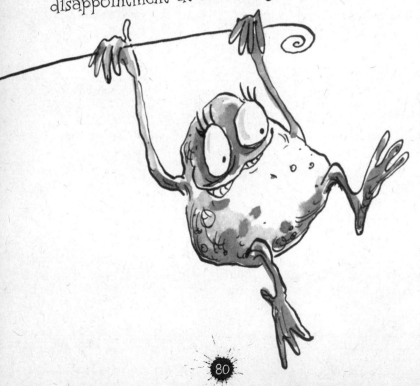

She tried not to hop with impatience and I tried not to twirl OFF my Lucky Whisker with excitement while we waited.

Finally, our wait was over. Last but not least, HA and Iodine took the stage and performed our

two

magma-hot

songs —

BE RIGHT THERE

and

STAR EXHIBIT.

I only wish you could have seen those Producers and Promoters and the rest of the audience when BACK IN BLACK had finished. They leapt to their feet. They wept. They clapped.

One PP cried out:

"IF EVER A GIRL BAND DESERVES TO BE BIGGER THAN THEIR DREAMS IT'S YOU!"

But this is where we hit rock bottom of the Trouble Abyss.

To fully understand why, go back to the EASY REVERSAL NOTE for that Look-Like-A-Girl-Band-Girl spell I invented — because reversal was

WHAT WAS about to happen!

"Now," said the first PP, pointing at HA. "You are Hagatha Agatha." Then pointing at Iodine, "and you are..."

At that moment THE MOON APPEARED AT A WINDOW.

Iodine glanced at it – SNEEZED THREE TIMES without knowing what she was doing – and answered the PP in all innocence:

"IODINE UNDERWOOD. THAT TIS I!"

And it WAS HER!

The Look-Like-A-Girl-Band-Girl spell reversed in a flash – and there was Iodine – a full-on High Hag.

At the sight of it, and her Girl Band
dreams going up in the smoke of truth,
HA fell down in a swoon.

Panic broke out in the Starstruck Room.

Though not for long: realising she was revealed to so many for what she is, Iodine went RIGHT OVER THE TOP with the Polished Talon Dust so no one would remember what they'd seen.

This time Bella and I escaped it by hiding under a chair — but a whole cloud fell on the helpless Haggy Aggy, swooning on the floor.
So much in fact that for two days she hasn't been able to remember her <u>own</u> name.

Of course, I'm taking great care
of her and feeding her Begoneberry
Broth to begone the effects of all that

Forgetfulness Dust.

I don't know what she will have to say when she fully recovers. I'm hoping she will remember everything and not give a gawbox that she nearly became a GALAXY-SIZED Girl Band. I'm hoping what happened in the Starstruck Room will teach her a lesson too about staying true to what you are — in her case a witch and a very good one, if only she'd be more willing.

As for me. I mean, I ask you. A GIRL BAND MANAGER? As I keep asking of myself in adazement: What WAS I thinking of? I'm a Highly Qualified Witch's Familiar from a long line of Witch's Familiars. That's what I am and that's what I always will be.

Mind you,

I don't see

why I can't be

that which I am —

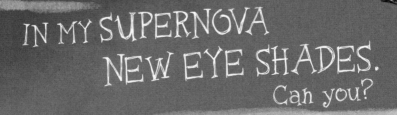

IN MY SUPERNOVA
NEW EYE SHADES.

Can you?

WITCHES' CHARTER
OF GOOD PRACTICE

1. Scare at least one child on the Other Side into his or her wits – every day (excellent), once in seven days (good), once a moon (average), once in two moons (bad), once in a blue moon (failed).

2. Identify any fully-grown Othersiders who were not properly scared into their wits as children and DO IT NOW. (It is never too late for a grown Othersider to come to his or her senses.)

3. Invent a new spell useful for every purpose and every occasion in the Witches' Calendar. Ensure you or your Familiar commits it to a Spell Book before it is lost to the Realms of Forgetfulness for ever.

4. Keep a proper witch's house at all times – filled with dust and spiders' webs, mould and earwigs underthings and ensure the jars on your kitchen shelves are always alive with good spell ingredients.

5. Cackle a lot. Cackling can be heard far and wide and serves many purposes such as (i) alerting others to your terrifying presence (ii) sounding hideous and thereby comforting to your fellow witches.

6. Make sure your Familiar keeps your means of proper travel (broomsticks) in good trim and that one, either or both of you exercise them regularly.

7. Never fail to present yourself anywhere and everywhere in full witch's uniform (i.e. black everything and no ribbons upon your hat ever). Sleeping in uniform is recommended as a means of saving dressing time.

8. Keep your Familiar happy with a good supply of Comfrey and Slime Buns. Remember, behind every great witch is a well-fed Familiar.

9. At all times acknowledge the authority of your local High Hags. As their eyes can do 360 degrees and they know everything there is to know, it is always in your interests to make their wishes your commands.

CONTRACT OF SERVICE

between
WITCH HAGATHA AGATHA, Haggy Aggy for short, HA for shortest
of Thirteen Chimneys, Wizton-under-Wold

&

the Witch's Familiar,
RUMBLEWICK SPELLWACKER MORTIMER B, RB for short

It is hereby agreed that, come
FIRE, Brimstone, CAULDRONS overflowing
or ALIEN WIZARDS invading,
for the NEXT SEVEN YEARS
RB will serve HA,
obey her EVERY WHIM and WORD and at all times assist her
in the ways of being a true and proper WITCH.

PAYMENT for services will be:
* a log basket to sleep in * unlimited Slime Buns for breakfast
* free use of HA's broomsticks (outside of peak brooming hours)
* and a cracked mirror for luck.

PENALTY for failing in his duties will be decided on the whim of
THE HAGS on HIGH.

SIGNED AND SEALED
this New Moon Day, 22nd of Remember

Haggy Aggy
....
Witch Hagatha Agatha

Rumblewick
....
Rumblewick Spellwacker Mortimer B

Trixie Fiddlestick
And witnessed by the High Hag, Trixie Fiddlestick

ORCHARD BOOKS

338 Euston Road, London NWI 3BH
Orchard Books Australia
Level 17/207 Kent Street, Sydney NSW 2000

ISBN: 978 I 84616 067 7

First published in 2007 by Orchard Books

A CIP catalogue record for this book is

available from the British Library.

Orchard Books is a division
of Hachette Children's Books

I 3 5 7 9 I0 8 6 4 2
Printed in China

To Lara and 'Ribbit
Ribbit' Gabe, with love
H.O.

For Jenny
S.W.

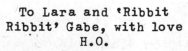

Dear Precious Children

The Publisher asked me to say something about these Diaries.
(As I do not write Otherside very well, I have dictated it to
the Publisher's Familiar/assistant. If she has not written it
down right, let me know and I'll turn her into a fat pumpkin.)

This is my message: I went to a lot of trouble to steal these
Diaries for you. And the Publisher gave me a lot of shoes in
exchange. If you do not read them the Publisher may want the
shoes back. So please, for my sake — the only witch in
witchdom who isn't willing to scare you for her own
entertainment — ENJOY THEM ALL.
Yours ever,

Haggy Aggy

Your fantabulous shoe-loving friend,
Hagatha Agatha (Haggy Aggy for short, HA for shortest) xx

ISBN 9781846160653

ISBN 9781846160691

ISBN 9781846160721

ISBN 9781846160714

ISBN 9781846160677

ISBN 9781846160660

ISBN 9781846160707

ISBN 9781846160684